Pete the Cat

STORYBOOK FAVORITES

GROOVY ADVENTURES

ISBN 978-0-06-286841-1

Typography by Lori Malkin Ehrlich
22 23 24 25 26 SAM 10 9 8 7 6 5 4 3 2 1

Pete the Cat
STORYBOOK FAVORITES

GROOVY ADVENTURES

by Kimberly & James Dean

HARPER
An Imprint of HarperCollinsPublishers

TABLE OF CONTENTS

Pete the Cat's
World Tour

Updated Edition

Pete and his bandmates are going on a world tour. They are ready to rock!

In Mexico, Pete and Gus practice for the show.

Uh-oh. Pete's belly starts to rumble.

Pete can't play if he's hungry! He needs something to eat.

CONCERT TONIGHT

"How about tacos?" suggests Gus.
He eats one filled with nopales. That's a kind of cactus.
Pete has a taco filled with fish, salsa, and lettuce.
Now he's ready to play!

9

The band's next concert is on a mountain in Peru.
Uh-oh. The air is a bit too chilly for Pete.
He can't play if he's cold. He needs to warm up!

"How about a cup of Peruvian hot chocolate?" asks a fan.

"I would love some," says Pete.

The hot chocolate tastes groovy and Pete feels warm.

Now he's ready to play!

11

The band's next stop is Iceland.
It is a long flight!
Uh-oh. Pete is sleepy.
He can't play if he's tired. He needs to relax!

Everyone takes a dip in the Blue Lagoon.
It is cold outside and hot in the lagoon. The water is very soothing.
"Ahhh, just what I needed," Pete says.
Now he's ready to play!

In France, Pete gets ready to play. But first, he wants a snack. Uh-oh. Pete can't decide if he should have a baguette or an éclair! If Pete doesn't make a choice, he will be late to the concert.

"Try both," says the baker.
"Merci," says Pete.
He eats his French treats in front of the Eiffel Tower.
Now he's ready to play!

15

The band practices in front of the Great Wall of China.
The long trip made Pete hungry.
Uh-oh. Pete can't play if he's thinking about food. He needs something to eat.

16

A local singer shows them to a restaurant.
Pete and the band eat dumplings with chopsticks.
Now he's ready to play!

17

In India, Pete tries to sing.
His throat is scratchy.
Uh-oh. Pete can't play if he's thirsty. He needs a drink.

Pete takes a sip of a cold mango lassi.
Yum!
Now he's ready to play!

The band's next stop is Egypt.
Uh-oh. The sand is too hot. It is burning Pete's feet.
He can't play if his feet hurt. He needs something to sit on.
A camel offers to let Pete sit on him.

Pete's feet do not hurt anymore. Now he's ready to play!

21

At Victoria Falls, Pete admires the waterfall.
It falls between Zambia and Zimbabwe.
"Cool!" Pete says. "We are in two countries at the same time."
Then Pete notices that the water is hitting his guitar.
Uh-oh. Pete can't play if his guitar is wet.
Squirrel has a plan. She finds an umbrella.

That's better.
Now Pete is ready to play.

The band's last stop is Trinidad.
Pete has no problems. He is ready to play.

The crowd goes wild.
"That was an amazing show," says Pete.
"I can't wait to come back."

25

The band's world tour is over. It is time to go home.
Pete loved his trip.

"The world is full of groovy places.
I can't wait to see them all!"

Pete the Cat

SUPER PETE

Pete the Cat is out for a walk.

Pete listens to the owls.

He listens to the frogs.

Just then, Pete hears a beep.

It is not coming from outside.

It is coming from his watch!

Pete races home.

It is time for Pete the Cat

to become Super Pete!

Pete presses a button in his room.

The wall slides away.

Pete sees a set of steps.

Down, down, down he goes.

Pete steps into his lair.
It is full of groovy things
to help him fight crime.

MOST
WANTED

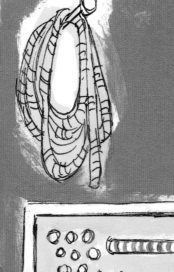

ME
1PUTER

Pete the Cat puts on
his awesome cat suit.
He puts on his cape
and his sneakers.

Now Super Pete is ready

to save the city.

Pete sees a flashing light.

There is a message

on his computer.

It is the mayor!

"Come quick, Super Pete,"

the mayor says.

"We need your help.

There is trouble at the warehouse."

Pete pulls a lever.

Whoosh!

Pete's nifty jet

sinks into his lair.

Pete hops into the jet.

He zips into the air.

Super Pete is on his way

to save the day!

Pete races through the sky.

He hits a button.

The jet shimmers.

The jet disappears.

Now the jet is invisible.

Now no one will know

Super Pete is coming.

Pete hovers over the warehouse.

He straps on a parachute.

He jumps.

Pete lands on the roof.

He goes inside the warehouse.

It is dark.

He cannot see.

Pete puts on his

night vision goggles.

He sees two bad guys.

They are carrying a box.

Pete picks up a rock.

He puts it in his slingshot.

The rock hits the box.

The bad guys drop the box.

They climb out of a window!

Pete races to the window.

The bad guys have a boat.

They are getting away!

Pete pushes a button

on his catsuit.

His sneakers turn into flippers.

A mask closes over his face.

Pete jumps into the water.

He swims after the bad guys.

Pete takes a rope

from his pocket.

He twirls it over his head.

Pete aims.

He throws.

The rope catches the boat.

Pete pulls himself
along the rope.

Pete climbs into

the bad guys' boat.

He ties up the bad guys.

Pete pushes a button

on his watch.

His jet appears above him.

Pete pulls the bad guys
into his jet.

Pete brings the bad guys

to the mayor.

Super Pete saved the day!

Pete the Cat
Checks Out the Library

Pete's mom is taking him to the library for the first time.
The librarian gives Pete his very own library card.
"Cool!" says Pete.
The librarian smiles. "Time for the tour."

The librarian takes Pete through the library.
There is a big desk where people wait to check out books.

59

The librarian takes Pete to her favorite room.
There are lots of Pete-size chairs and tables and shelves.
There are books of every shape, size, and color.

"What do I do now?" Pete asks.
"Now you read a book," the librarian says.
"Which book should I read?" asks Pete.
"You can read any book you like," says the librarian.

Pete looks around. There are so many books!
Finally he picks one about jets and airplanes.

He reads it and pretends he is a stunt pilot.
He flies a superfast jet and does loop-the-
loops and spirals high in the sky!

Then Pete finds a book with dragons,
wizards, and unicorns on the cover.

He reads it and imagines that he is a powerful wizard, using magic spells and a special wand to defend his castle against a fire-breathing dragon.

Next Pete opens a book about spiders and insects. He reads it and imagines that he is a scientist studying all types of critters in the wild.

He has to be very still to study some critters . . .

and very fast to study others.

Then Pete chooses a book with all sorts of scary monsters on the cover. It is a book of fairy tales.

Pete reads it and pretends that he is in a dark, spooky forest trying to outsmart a big, bad wolf.

Pete puts that book back on the shelf—it is too scary!

69

Pete opens up a book about the pyramids in Egypt.
He reads it and pretends that he is an explorer
riding a camel across the desert . . .

and climbing to the top of a giant pyramid.

Next Pete picks a book with all sorts of robots on the cover.
He reads it and imagines that he is a robot at a robot dance party.

72

His arms and legs make whizzing sounds when he moves. When Robot Pete speaks, he says,

"Bleep. Bloop. Bleep!"

Next Pete picks up a book about superheroes.
He reads it and makes believe that he is a superhero.

He flies around the city in a colorful cape
chasing bad guys and saving the day.

Then Pete spots a big book about the ocean and all its creatures.

He reads it and imagines that he is a scientist in a submarine deep in the Atlantic Ocean, looking for whales, squids, and sharks.

76

There are so many wonderful books to read at the library.
Pete can be whatever he imagines with a book.

Reading is super groovy!

Pete ^{the} Cat's
TRIP TO THE SUPERMARKET

Pete and Bob are hungry
after a big day of fun
at the park.

"Dad, can we have a snack?"

Bob asks.

Dad checks
the fridge.

Dad checks
the pantry.

Dad checks
the secret
snack nook.

"We need to buy groceries,"

says Dad.

Dad starts to make a list.
"We need milk and eggs
and fish and chicken."

"I want raspberries," says Bob.

"I want apples," says Pete.

Pete, Bob, and Dad

make a long list

and take it to the supermarket.

Oh no!

The wind blows the list

out of Dad's hands.

"It's cool," says Pete.

"I remember the list."

"I do too," says Bob.

First they stop in aisle ten.

The sign says "Dairy."

"We need milk," says Pete.

"And cheese," says Bob.

"The stinky kind."

Next they go to aisle nine.

"Yum," says Dad.

"I love bacon!"

"Don't forget the chicken,"

says Pete.

They almost pass aisle eight
when Pete remembers eggs.

"Regular or jumbo?" asks Pete.

"Jumbo," says Dad.

"Groovy," says Pete.

Bob can't pick between
straight and curvy noodles
in aisle seven.

"How about bow ties?"

asks Dad.

"Awesome," says Bob.

Aisle six smells fruity.

"Remember the apples," says Pete.

"Remember the raspberries," says

Bob.

In aisle five,

Dad tastes a hot dog.

Yummy!

In aisle four,

Pete tastes a cupcake.

Sweet!

Dad lets Pete and Bob

choose a treat in aisle three.

Pete picks crackers
shaped like fish.

Bob picks popcorn.

Brrrr! It is cold in aisle two.

Dad puts mango popsicles
in the cart.

Aisle one has
sunflowers, tulips,
and blue daisies.

Pete and Bob pick tulips

for Grandma.

"She'll love them," says Dad.

"I think we got everything
except the fish!" says Dad.
But their car is packed
with yummy treats.
Next time!

STRAWBERRY
ICE CREAM

JUMBO
DINOSAUR EGGS

FISH
CRACKERS

POP-
CORN

MILK

Pete the Cat
and the
Supercool Science Fair

Pete cannot wait for Friday.
His school is having a science fair!

110

Pete has never been a scientist.
Now he can try it out!

111

Pete's teacher tells the students they will do experiments in groups.

Pete is in a group with Callie, Gus, and Squirrel.
"Our experiment is going to be groovy," says Pete.
"What should we do?"

"Let's build a mini submarine,"
says Callie.

"Or grow a giant tree,"
says Squirrel.

"Or invent an invisible guitar,"
says Pete.

"Why don't we make a volcano?" asks Gus.

"Woah," they all say. "Volcanoes are awesome."

The group plans the experiment at Pete's house.
His mom brings them snacks.

"Would any scientist like a cookie?" she asks.
They all raise their hands.
The cookies are warm and gooey.

The scientists check the **BIG BOOK OF EXPERIMENTS** for materials. They need glue, water, newspaper, paint, and a plastic bottle for the volcano.

They need vinegar, baking soda, liquid dish soap, and a secret ingredient for the lava.

Pete and Gus mix the glue and water.

Squirrel and Callie tear the newspaper into strips.

They cover the plastic bottle with glue and paper.
It looks like a sticky white volcano!

Oh no!
The paint in the brown bottle is blue.
"What are we going to do?" Callie asks.
They can't find brown paint anywhere.

"That's pretty cool," says Pete. "Maybe it's okay that we have a blue volcano."
"We'll be the only group with a blue volcano," says Squirrel.

"Let's test the lava so we know the volcano will erupt at the science fair," Pete says.
Gus pours baking soda and liquid dish soap into the volcano, and Callie adds vinegar.

Nothing happens . . . at first.

All of a sudden, a lot of lava starts coming out. "Supercool!" says Callie.

The team high-five each other. But the lava is still coming out. Soon it is a huge mess.

"Oh, Mom isn't going to be happy," says Pete.

At least the scientists are ready for the fair on Friday!

When Pete and his team arrive at the fair, they see all the other groovy experiments. They all look awesome.

Grumpy Toad and Octopus grew rock candy in jars!

Emma and Marty made slime!

"We don't stand a chance," says Gus.
"Don't worry. We have the secret ingredient,"
says Pete.

At the science fair, Pete's teacher loves the blue volcano.
"Wait till you see it erupt," Pete says.

The whole class watches Callie pour vinegar into the volcano.

131

A second later, **glitter** lava gushes out. Everyone cheers!

The scientists cheer the loudest.

133

"Science experiments are hard work," says Pete. "But being on an awesome team makes them a whole lot easier!"

COOLEST EXPERIMENT at the SCIENCE FAIR

Pete ^{the} Cat's

FAMILY ROAD TRIP

Pete, Bob, Mom, and Dad
are going on a road trip
across the United States!

Dad loads the bags onto the roof.

Mom picks the music.

Bob and Pete grab the bike.

The first stop is Niagara Falls.

They ride a boat

to see the waterfall up close.

Pete loves pretending he's the captain.

CAT of the MIST

Next stop is Boston!

The family walks the Freedom Trail.

They take a photo

in front of Paul Revere's house.

"Historic and cool," says Bob.

Now they are off to a new city.

It is New York City!

The family takes an elevator

to the top of One World Trade Center.

"Look, it's the Statue of Liberty,"

says Dad.

In Savannah, they ride a riverboat.

Pete orders a slice of peach pie.

"Yum," says Pete.

"Life is good."

When they arrive at Key West,

Pete meets a six-toed cat.

"Your paws are groovy," says Pete.

"Right back at you," says the cat.

New Orleans is famous
for jazz music.

The groovy jazz music makes
everyone dance in the streets!

Everyone is excited about the next stop.

But then . . . uh-oh!

The car gets a flat tire on Route 66.

"Don't worry," says Mom.

"We can't let this ruin our trip!"

Mom and Dad change the tire.

Soon the family is on their way again!

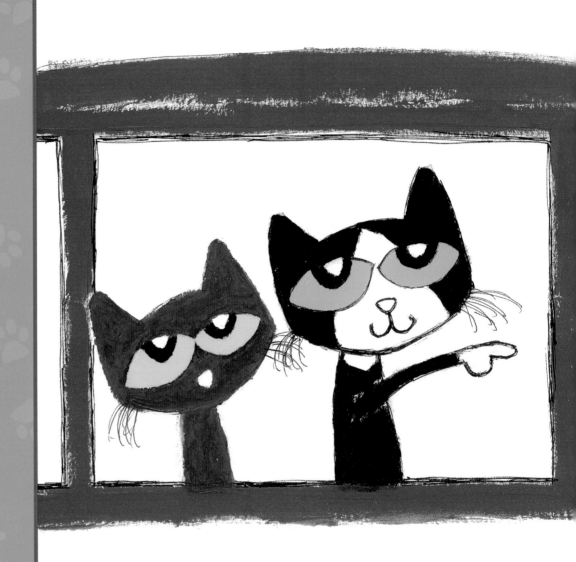

Mom parks the car.

"Look over there," says Bob.

It's Mount Rushmore.

What a sight to see!

The family stops to take a photo.

At Yellowstone National Park,

everyone unwinds.

The park is so pretty and peaceful.

Bob sees bison snacking on grass.

"Check out those horns," says Mom.

Suddenly, Old Faithful shoots water

high into the air.

"Cool," says Pete.

Bob thinks it's time to try something different than a car ride.

The family goes on a horse ride instead

in Utah's Monument Valley!

In Los Angeles, Pete checks out

The Cat Hollywood Walk of Fame.

Pete puts his paws in the pawprints.

"I feel like a star," he says.

When they get to San Francisco,

they all squeeze into a cable car.

Pete stands in the front and says,

"Toot!"

The last stop is Seattle.

They go to the top of the Space Needle.

"Wow," says Mom.

"This city is pretty at night."

Finally it is time to go home.

"We saw so many cool places,"

says Bob.

"What was your favorite part

of the road trip?" asks Mom.

Pete thinks long and hard.

There were so many neat sights.

"The best part was being together

with you all," says Pete.

Pete the Cat

SECRET AGENT

Look!

Can you spot Secret Agent Meow?
He's the coolest spy in town. No one knows that
Agent Meow's true identity is Pete the Cat. Not even Bob!

Agent Meow is an expert at solving cases.

Last year, he caught the Ruby Robber.

"My favorite necklace!"

Two weeks ago, he found the missing key to town.

"You've saved the town again!"

Experimental Rocket

CAT

Hidden Elevator

Escape Hatch

Exit Tunnel

Meow-Mobile

Laboratory and Spy Gadgets

Snack Room

Skateboard Practice Room

Agent Meow works in a top secret location. The only way to unlock his door is with his pawprint.

Inside his headquarters, he has a lot of very groovy gadgets.

AGENT MEOW'S UNDERGROUND HEADQUARTERS

The meow-mobile can take Agent Meow anywhere at lightning speed.

It can turn into a car, a helicopter,

and even a skateboard.

Agent Meow also has a supercool spy watch camera. It looks like an ordinary watch. But with one click, it's anything but ordinary.

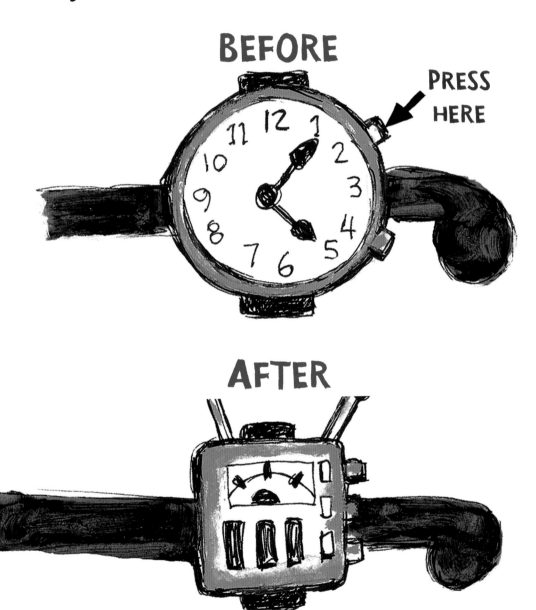

BEFORE

PRESS HERE

AFTER

He just created his own flying listening device so he can hear everything, even when he's not nearby.

He calls it his secret-catcher.

Sometimes when Agent Meow is on a mission, he wears a disguise.

Once, Agent Meow coated himself in paint to blend into a painting.

Another time, he pretended to be a tree.
A bird family built a nest on his head.
He's a cat undercover!

173

One morning, Agent Meow is flying his secret-catcher when he hears a surprising message.

Agent Meow can't tell who is talking because there is too much static, but he hears:

"Supersecret rendezvous . . . Seven p.m. tonight . . . You know where to meet."

Agent Meow is very intrigued.

He needs to fine-tune his secret-catcher so he can hear better next time. He heads to the hardware store. He takes a shortcut through the park.

Time is of the essence when you're a spy!

Agent Meow spots a group of his friends whispering by the swings.

Why would anyone come to the park and not play on the swings? he wonders.

He disguises himself as a dog so he can get closer.

"Tonight is going to be huge," says Squirrel.
"I really hope we can pull it off," says Octopus.
"What should I bring?"

"Go ask Grumpy Toad," says Squirrel.
"He knows the plan."

Grumpy Toad works at
the library!
   Agent Meow knows
exactly where to go next.

The library is very quiet, so Agent Meow tiptoes around the bookshelves.

Good thing he knows a secret hiding spot inside the bookcase!

Agent Meow pulls on his favorite book, and it leads to an underground hideaway.
Finally he spots Grumpy Toad whispering to Gus.
He pulls out his secret-catcher.

"Do we need anything else for tonight?"

"No, that's all right. Turtle is already at the market. He's picking up stuff for me."

Agent Meow knows he will never make it to
the market before Turtle leaves.
At least not without his meow-mobile!

Whoosh!

"Aha! Suspect Turtle spotted," says Agent Meow. "Looks like he is buying gallons of banana ice cream. . . . But why is Callie there, too?"

Agent Meow turns on his secret-catcher. He hears Callie and Turtle talking.

"I found **Grumpy Toad's** fish sticks."

"**Cool**, now let's get going. We can't be late to **Gus's** house."

Agent Meow checks his watch.
He has to move fast!
He hops onto his meow-mobile and ZOOMS over.

Whoosh!

It's only ten minutes until it's seven p.m!

What could the secret meeting be about? Agent Meow wonders.
He'll need the perfect disguise—one that will blend in.

He tries on several hats . . .

glasses . . .

and even a wig.

Suddenly he gets the perfect idea. He will go as Pete the Cat! No one will expect him.

Agent Meow tries to whistle and act cool as he walks by Gus's house.

Yet he can't help but feel a little nervous.
He walks up to the house. It seems quiet. Too quiet.

"**Surprise!**" everyone yells.

"It's a surprise birthday party for you!" says Callie. "We got all your favorite foods, like fish sticks and banana ice cream."

FISH STICKS

HAPPY BIRTHDAY

"How did you know it was my birthday?" asks Agent Meow.
"You can't keep a secret from us," says Gus.

Pete the Cat may be able to keep his secret identity, Agent Meow, hidden from his friends, but he definitely can't keep his birthday a secret.

"This is best surprise party of all time!"